# ATTENTION, READER!

This is a story about the Ghostwriter team, an amusement park, and a mysterious clown. As you read it, it's up to *you* to decide where the Ghostwriter team and I should go next. At the end of every chapter you'll be given a choice.

It's also up to you to help the team solve the puzzles they find. Sometimes you'll need the answer to one puzzle before you can solve another. And sometimes the answer to a puzzle will be important later on in the story.

To keep track of the clues you find, start a Ghostwriter casebook. Just take a piece of paper and write down all of the clues you discover and all of the places the team visits. That way you'll be sure not to forget anything important.

Are you ready to begin? Then let's go!

—GHOSTWRITER

JOIN THE TEAM!

Do you watch GHOSTWRITER on PBS? Then you know that when you read and write to solve a mystery or unravel a puzzle, you're using the same smarts and skills the GHOSTWRITER team uses.

We hope you'll join the team and read along to help solve the mysterious and puzzling goings-on in these GHOSTWRITER books!

Amazement Park Adventure

Richie Chevat

Illustrated by Lennie Peterson

A CHILDREN'S TELEVISION WORKSHOP BOOK

BANTAM BOOKS
NEW YORK · TORONTO · LONDON · SYDNEY · AUCKLAND

AMAZEMENT PARK ADVENTURE

A Bantam Book / February 1994

Ghostwriter, Gh•st writer and ☄
are trademarks of Children's Television Workshop.
All rights reserved. Used under authorization.
Art direction by Marva Martin.
Cover design by Susan Herr.
Illustrations by Lennie Peterson.

ISBN 0-553-48091-X

Published simultaneously in the United States and Canada

Bantam Books are published by Bantam Books, a division of
Bantam Doubleday Dell Publishing Group, Inc. Its trademark,
consisting of the words "Bantam Books" and the portrayal of a
rooster, is Registered in U.S. Patent and Trademark Office and in
other countries. Marca Registrada. Bantam Books, 1540 Broadway,
New York, New York 10036.

PRINTED IN THE UNITED STATES OF AMERICA

BAW 0 9 8 7 6 5 4 3 2

"What's wrong, Jamal?" asks Alex.

It's a warm spring day. Jamal and the other members of the Ghostwriter team are at Coney Island, standing in front of Jesse's Fun House—their favorite amusement park attraction.

"Look!" Jamal points to a large sign and reads it out loud. "Jesse's Fun House—Out of Business for Good."

Rob tries the gate to the Fun House. It's locked.

"That's weird," he mutters. "Jesse wouldn't just leave Coney Island. He must be around. How can we find him?"

"We can leave him a note," Tina offers. She takes her Ghostwriter pen from around her neck and starts to write on a piece of paper from her notebook.

Dear Jesse,
We came by to see you, but the Fun House was closed. Where did you go?

Suddenly a sparkling ball of light zips through the air. The letters of Tina's note start to glow. "Ghostwriter!" she gasps. Everyone crowds in to see what's happening.

Ghostwriter is the team's mysterious, ghostly friend. They don't know who he is or where he came from. He can't hear or see, but he can read anything—anywhere. He often uses the letters he finds around him to send messages to the team.

This time, when he's finished moving around the letters on Tina's note, his message reads: JESSE'S HOT DOGS.

"Jesse's hot dogs?" Tina reads it out loud. "What's that? What's Ghostwriter reading?"

"Look!" Rob points down the block to a crowd around a food stand. The team races over and finds Jesse leaning over the counter, selling hot dogs.

"Hi, kids," Jesse calls. "Glad to see you." He's a tall, thin man with dark brown skin and a black mustache.

"We're glad to see *you*. But why'd you close the Fun House?" Lenni asks.

"I had to." Jesse sighs. "I had no customers. Everyone started going to Ride-O-Rama." He points across the street to a flashy-looking amusement park, covered with neon lights. A long line of kids is waiting to get in.

"Ride-O-Rama's a dump!" says Alex.

"Not anymore," Jesse replies. "Some guy named Woolcott bought it and put a lot of money into it. Now it's the hottest place in Coney Island."

"Why don't you do the same thing?" asks Jamal.

"I don't have the money," Jesse says sadly. "If only I knew where Klondike's treasure is hidden."

"Who's Klondike?" asks Rob.

"Klondike the Clown," Lenni explains. "He made a fortune selling clown supplies. You know, rubber noses and huge clown shoes, stuff like that. All this used to belong to him, including the Fun House and Ride-O-Rama."

"Even this hot-dog stand," adds Jesse. "Klondike was my best friend. He left me his fortune when he died. The only problem is, I can't find the money. It's hidden around here somewhere. But whenever I asked Klondike where he put it, he'd just say, 'My fortune is in my shoes.' And then he'd wiggle those giant red shoes of his."

Rob shakes his head. "Wow. And now you have no idea where the money is. Too bad."

Lenni looks at her friends. "I bet *we* could find it."

"Yeah!" Alex is psyched. "It's like this mystery I read once. We'll call it 'The Case of Klondike's Cash.'"

"Great," says Jamal. "But where do we start? Coney Island is a big place."

"To find the treasure, we need to know more about Klondike," Tina points out. "Jesse, where did he hang out?"

"Two places," Jesse answers. "At his office in Ride-O-Rama and here at the hot-dog stand. He loved hot dogs."

Alex turns toward Ride-O-Rama. "We should start at his office. He must have left clues there."

"Yeah! Let's figure out a cover story to get in," says Gaby. "I don't think we should tell Mr. Woolcott why we want to look around."

"Wait," Lenni interrupts. "Maybe Klondike left some clues right here. After all, Jesse says he loved hot dogs."

Alex looks around the stand. There's a counter, a few tables, and not much else. "No way there's anything hidden here. I say we go to Ride-O-Rama."

Everyone agrees, except for Lenni. "I don't know," she says. "Maybe we're missing something."

Should the team go to Ride-O-Rama? Or is Lenni right? Is there a clue hidden in the hot-dog stand? Here's a puzzle to help you decide. Unscramble the words in capital letters and write them in the blank spaces. The circled letters will spell out a clue to what the team should do.

IF YOU THINK THE TEAM SHOULD GO TO RIDE-O-RAMA, TURN TO CHAPTER 13, PAGE 41 AFTER YOU'VE COMPLETED THE PUZZLE.

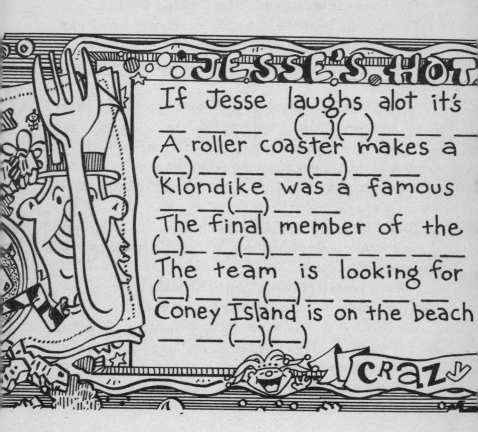

JESSE'S HOT

If Jesse laughs alot it's
— — — — (_)(_) — — — —
A roller coaster makes a
(_) — — — — — (_) — —
Klondike was a famous
— — (_) — — — — —
The final member of the
(_) — — (_) — — — — — —
The team is looking for
(_) — — — (_) — —
Coney Island is on the beach
— — (_)(_)

CRAZY

IF YOU THINK THE TEAM SHOULD STAY AT THE HOT-DOG STAND, TURN TO CHAPTER 9, PAGE 28 AFTER YOU'VE COMPLETED THE PUZZLE.

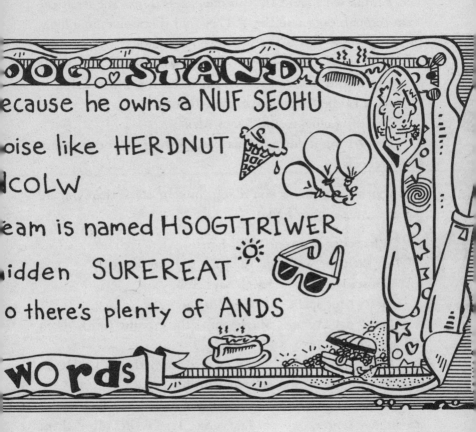

...OG...STAND...

ecause he owns a NUF SEOHU

oise like HERDNUT

lcOLW

eam is named HSOGTTRIWER

idden SUREREAT

o there's plenty of ANDS

wOrds

"I think we should try this one," says Tina. She leads the team through door number 4. They find themselves in a long, curving, brightly lit white hall. Even the floor is white.

"Hey, what's that written on the wall?" asks Jamal. He points to a bold black message painted on the white wall.

"It's a riddle!" Gaby says immediately.

"No, it's a clue, stupid," says Alex.

"I'm writing it down," Tina says, copying the message into her notebook.

3. If you win a prize or you're tops in your class, then you are the _____ one of all.

"What does it mean?" asks Jamal.

Just then the words on the page start to dance.

"Ghostwriter has an idea," says Rob.

Ghostwriter spells the word *best*.

"Best?" says Lenni. "Maybe that's the missing word. 'Then you are the *best* one of all.' "

"Look," calls Gaby, who's moved down the hall. "Here's another sentence with a missing word!"

Quickly the team moves along the hall. They find one of the strange sentences every few yards. Tina writes all of them down. They follow the curve of the hall until they're standing in front of a gleaming white door.

"Let's see what's inside," Rob says. He turns the knob and the door swings open. "Whoa! Intense!" he gasps.

The room beyond is perfectly round. The floor is made up

of black and white squares in a strange pattern. The walls are striped with wavy black and white lines. And the ceiling is painted with a huge black and white spiral.

"Wow," Lenni says. "This room is making me seasick."

The team walks in, and Jamal lets the door swing closed behind him. As it clicks shut, there's a soft hum. Then the floor of the room slowly starts to spin!

"Now I *know* I'm going to be sick," Lenni moans. "Let's get out of here!"

"Hold up!" Alex points to the floor. "Those black and white squares there look like a crossword puzzle! See, the white squares are numbered."

Jamal snaps his fingers. "Hey, I bet the sentences in the hallway are clues for this puzzle."

"Yeah!" Rob adds. "The missing words are the answers!"

"Maybe," Tina says, scratching her head. "But Ghostwriter said the first missing word was *best,* and that doesn't fit in the puzzle. There must be a trick to it."

"We can crack it!" Gaby declares.

"Not if I throw up first," Lenni mutters.

"Okay, we have to think fast," says Jamal. "We have to figure out the trick and solve this puzzle!"

There *is* a trick to this crossword puzzle. The answers to the questions aren't the answers that go into the puzzle. You have to change them somehow. If you need a hint, go back to Chapter 9, page 28 and solve the puzzle there.

When you've figured out the trick, fill in the crossword puzzle. Then look at the shaded boxes. Unscramble those letters to spell out a word for the puzzle in Klondike's Cavern. (Hint: What do people sit on?)

ONCE YOU'VE COMPLETED THE PUZZLE, WRITE DOWN THE ANSWER AND TURN TO CHAPTER 6, PAGE 20.

ACROSS

3. If you win a prize or you're tops in your class, then you are the _____ one of all.
4. Before the lion tamer begins, he takes _____ his cape.
5. If a tightrope walker slips, he falls _____ .
6. Some clowns wear padding to make themselves look _____ .
7. When you swim at Coney Island, you get all_____.
9. It's funny to see ten clowns squeeze into a _____ car.
10. Pickles and lemons taste _____ .

DOWN

1. They say Santa Claus lives at the _____ Pole.
2. The race starter calls, "Ready, set, _____ !"
5. Trapeze artists swing around high _____ our heads.
8. You have to be _____ on your feet to be a good acrobat.

SWOOSH! CLICK!

As soon as the team steps through the opening in the wall, the panel slides shut behind them.

"Hey! It's locked!" Rob rattles the door handle. "I can't budge it."

"Great," Gaby says. "What do we do now? Yell for help?"

Lenni shakes her head. "Only Mr. Woolcott will hear us and I don't want to ask *him* for help. Does anyone have a flashlight?"

"I do," says Alex. "Detectives always carry one."

Gaby snickers. "Since when are you a detective?"

"Give me a break," Alex grumbles. He switches the flashlight on and they see that they're at the end of a long tunnel that slopes downward.

"Look!" Gaby points to a message written on the side of the tunnel. It says:

Klondike's Cavern. My fortune came from clowns. It can only be found by someone who likes FUN. If you like FUN, then step right in!

"The treasure!" Lenni grins. "I knew it was in here. Come on." She heads down the tunnel, guided by the light of Alex's flashlight. The rest of the team follows.

• •

Down they go until the tunnel ends in a large, gloomy room. There are six doors leading from the room. Five have the numbers from one to five written on them in red. The sixth door has the word FINISH written on it. On the opposite wall is a large portrait of a clown. His costume is decorated with letters in a big gridlike pattern.

"That must be a picture of Klondike," says Rob.

"Yeah, and look at that costume," Jamal stares at the picture. "What are all the letters for?"

"It looks like a word search," says Gaby. "You know, where you have to find the hidden words and circle them."

"I'm making a copy of it in my notebook," says Tina, busily writing. "I'm sure we can't find the treasure until we solve this puzzle."

"But what are the hidden words?" asks Lenni. "Some are listed, but there are five dotted lines under the drawing. I bet those are for five extra hidden words that aren't listed."

Alex frowns. "We can't solve the puzzle unless we know what all the words are."

"Hey!" Jamal's eyes open wide. "Maybe the missing words are behind those doors."

"Maybe we should check it out," Rob agrees, nodding.

Gaby shivers. "Maybe we should get out of here. This place gives me the creeps!"

TURN TO CHAPTER 6, PAGE 20.

"Let's try door number one," says Alex. "I bet there's a clue behind there."

He opens the door slowly. The rusty hinges creak.

"No one's come through here in a long time," says Gaby, who's standing right behind her brother. "Creepy!"

On the other side of the door is a narrow flight of stairs. One by one, the team goes through the door and up the stairs. They walk into a room lit by an eerie blue light.

"Yeow!" Tina yells. "What's that?"

She's staring at someone who looks about ten feet tall with giant legs as thick as tree trunks.

After a second Lenni bursts out laughing. "Tina! It's you— in a trick mirror. This is the Hall of Mirrors."

Everybody laughs. Gaby and Lenni start making faces in the mirrors.

Jamal waves his hands. "Chill, you guys," he calls. "We're here to find a clue."

"But I don't see any clues," says Tina.

"What about this writing on the wall?" Rob asks.

Lenni squints at the wall. "Doesn't look like writing to me. It's just some weird scratches."

"Hey!" Alex cries. "I bet it's mirror writing! See, it's backward until you look at it in a mirror. These words must be part of the puzzle."

Can you help the team solve the puzzle? Look at the picture of Klondike the Clown at the top of the page. Then look at the reflections in the mirrors. Only one is the exact mirror image of Klondike's picture. Which is it? Circle it and hold the page up to a mirror. The word under the circled reflection is one of the missing words for the puzzle in Klondike's Cavern.

WRITE DOWN THE ANSWER AND TURN TO CHAPTER 6, PAGE 20.

AROUSEL CARNIVAL TIGER

SEALS STILTS JUGGLER

"This door must lead to the treasure," says Jamal.

They all file out through the door marked FINISH into a dark tunnel.

SCRAPE! SCRAPE!

"What's that?" Tina whispers nervously.

"It's coming from up ahead," Jamal whispers back.

They follow the tunnel for a long way. Finally they come to a large, dark basement. The walls are made of old cement blocks and rusted pipes run overhead. One bare light bulb casts mysterious shadows everywhere.

SCRAPE! SCRAPE!

The noise is coming from the other side of a large boiler. Carefully the team tiptoes around to look.

"Mr. Woolcott!" Tina exclaims.

Mr. Woolcott whirls to face the team, in shock. Beads of sweat are running down his face. His clothes are dirty and he's hiding something behind his back.

"What are you kids doing here?" he demands.

"*Us?*" Lenni retorts. "What are *you* doing here? This is Jesse's property. Look at the boiler."

A paper tag on the boiler reads "Jesse's Fun House."

"Oh," Mr. Woolcott says in a much friendlier tone. "I guess I got lost. These tunnels are confusing. You could get lost, too. Why don't you let me lead you out?"

Suddenly something behind him drops with a clang.

Lenni runs around Mr. Woolcott. "A shovel!" she cries. "And a hole! He's been digging for Klondike's treasure."

"You know about the treasure?" Mr. Woolcott's eyes narrow.

"Yes," says Jamal. "And we also know you can't dig here. This place still belongs to Jesse."

"We're going to tell him what you're up to," says Gaby.

"Big deal," Mr. Woolcott sneers. He heads for a stairway that leads up out of the basement. "*You'll* never find the treasure. That map is screwy!"

With that, he turns and stomps up the stairs.

Rob frowns. "What did he mean about a map?"

"Maybe this one," Alex calls. He's studying a large piece of paper that's taped to the wall. It's a map of Jesse's Fun House. Next to each of the attractions is a big number with a circle around it.

"Hey, this is it! This map tells where the treasure is buried," says Gaby. "We did it! We found the treasure!"

"Calm down. We haven't found it yet," Jamal tells her. "This map doesn't say anything about treasure. And I don't think it's going to be that simple. After all, Mr. Woolcott just said the map is screwy."

"Maybe there's a clue somewhere—a number that matches one of the numbers on the map," Rob says.

"Look!" Tina cries. "On the map there's a little story about Klondike. Weird—I don't get it." She writes a note in her book: "What does the story mean?"

Ghostwriter's glow flies over Tina's note, then over the map. Suddenly letters on the map start to jump around.

"Look!" Alex whispers. "Ghostwriter's sending us a message."

The letters on the map settle into this message:
THERE ARE MANY NUMBERS HERE.

"We know there are many numbers," Lenni complains. "But which numbers tell us where the treasure is buried?"

"Wait a minute." Jamal holds up a hand. "Maybe Ghostwriter means the numbers in the story about Klondike."

"I don't see any numbers," Rob says.

"Sure," says Jamal, grinning. "They're written out as words. And I bet they form some kind of secret message."

Here's the story and the map that's on the wall of the basement. Can you help the team solve the puzzle and find the place where the treasure is hidden?

First, write down all of the words in the story that are in CAPITAL LETTERS. Can you figure out what to do with the numbers? When you're done, you should have one number as your answer.

Now use that number to find the place on the map where the treasure is hidden. Hint: If you finished the puzzle in Klondike's Cavern, you'll know how to find the right place on the map.

Do you know where the treasure is hidden?

IF YOU THINK THE TEAM SHOULD GO TO THE WAX MUSEUM, TURN TO CHAPTER 7, PAGE 22.

IF YOU THINK THE TEAM SHOULD GO TO THE ROLLER COASTER, TURN TO CHAPTER 12, PAGE 40.

When Klondike the Clown was TWO, he AND his THREE brothers lost a toy clown. You could say they were MINUS ONE clown.

But Klondike grew up to be a clown after practicing lots of TIMES. SEVEN years later he was very famous, PLUS he owned FIVE properties in Coney Island.

Here's the puzzle on the wall of Klondike's Cavern.

1. Find and circle every word on the list below the drawing. Words may go up, down, across, backward, or diagonally.
2. There are five words missing from the list. Look for the missing words behind the doors. Each time the team comes back to this room, they should have another word to add to the list.
3. When you've found all five missing words, circle them on the puzzle. There should be some letters left over.
4. Write down the leftover letters. They form a clue for later in the story.

If you've finished the puzzle, the team is ready to go through the door marked FINISH.

IF YOU THINK THE TEAM SHOULD GO THROUGH THE DOOR MARKED FINISH, TURN TO CHAPTER 5, PAGE 15. IF YOU THINK THE TEAM SHOULD GO THROUGH DOOR 1, TURN TO CHAPTER 4, PAGE 12. IF YOU THINK THE TEAM SHOULD GO THROUGH DOOR 2, TURN TO CHAPTER 11, PAGE 36. IF YOU THINK THE TEAM SHOULD GO THROUGH DOOR 3, TURN TO CHAPTER 10, PAGE 32. IF YOU THINK THE TEAM SHOULD GO THROUGH DOOR 4, TURN TO CHAPTER 2, PAGE 6. IF YOU THINK THE TEAM SHOULD GO THROUGH DOOR 5, TURN TO CHAPTER 8, PAGE 24.

E L E P H A N T
P R E T G V W R
O O N E N R O A
R E P S I E L P
T S U C R I C E
H T M A O A P Z
G A N U N R M E
I E B D E R N S
T S Y P M I H C
L E S U O R A C

CLOWN ELEPHANT _____
CIRCUS _____ TENT
_____ _____ RING
CANDY _____ TRAPEZE

7

"Thirty-one," says Gaby. "But remember the clue in Klondike's Cavern? We have to reverse the numbers. That makes it thirteen—the wax museum!"

"What are we waiting for?" asks Alex. "Let's go!"

"I'm going to get Jesse," Rob calls. He heads off to find their friend.

In a few minutes the team is inside the Fun House's wax museum. The long room is lined with dozens of life-size wax statues of all sorts of famous people. Alex spots a statue of Sherlock Holmes. The famous detective is peering at a scrap of paper through a magnifying glass.

"Hey, what's up, Homey?" Alex asks. "Get it? Homey?"

"Ooh, Alex, that's lame," Lenni says, laughing.

"Hey, we have work to do, guys. Only . . . " Jamal gazes around the huge room. "Where do we start?"

Gaby picks up a brochure from a stack by the door. "Maybe Ghostwriter can help." She takes her Ghostwriter pen from around her neck and writes across the brochure: "Where would Klondike hide his treasure? Any ideas?"

Ghostwriter's glow moves across Gaby's note. Then it disappears inside the brochure. A moment later the whole thing glows with a pulsing light.

Gaby opens the brochure. Inside is a list of all of the statues in the wax museum. Ghostwriter's glow lights up a name on the list. #36: KLONDIKE THE CLOWN, it says.

"Hey, yeah! Why didn't *I* think of that?" Alex says, slapping his forehead. "The statue of Klondike! Of course he'd hide his fortune somewhere near his own statue!"

The kids rush down the hall to the wax statue of Klondike the Clown. "There it is," Tina says, panting. "Now where's the treasure?"

"I bet I know," says a familiar voice.

"Jesse!" everyone shouts.

Jesse and Rob come running down the hall.

"I should have figured this out myself," says Jesse. "Klondike was always in here—especially late at night."

"So where's the treasure?" Rob asks. "In the statue?"

"Sort of," Jesse answers with a smile. "I think it's here." He bends down and peels back the bright red shoes from the statue's giant feet. A gleam of gold appears.

"Gold!" Tina whispers.

"His feet are solid gold," Jamal says. "Wow!"

Jesse laughs. "He always said his fortune was in his shoes. Now I know he really meant it!"

THE END—YOU DID IT!

"I like the looks of this one," says Rob. The rest of the team follows him through door number 5.

Rob leads them up a flight of stairs and they come out into a baseball-toss arcade. People are lined up along a counter throwing balls at targets in the shape of ducks, ships, planes, elephants, and other things. On each target is a letter.

"I bet I can hit any target," Alex boasts.

"What good will that do?" asks Tina. "We're looking for a clue."

Gaby rolls her eyes. "He's just a show-off."

Alex's ears turn red.

"Maybe there's a pattern in the targets," Jamal suggests. "Let's write them down and ask Ghostwriter if he sees anything."

Tina copies down all of the letters on the targets and then writes, "These letters were on the targets. We're looking for a pattern."

Everyone peers over Tina's shoulder. After a moment Ghostwriter rearranges the letters in her notebook.

I DON'T SEE ONE. MAYBE THE PATTERN IS NOT IN THE LETTERS, he writes.

• •

"Not in the letters?" Lenni repeats. "Where else could it be?"

"Every target is a different shape," Jamal notes. "Maybe the shapes are a pattern."

The team stares at the targets for a while. Then Lenni sighs. "If there's any kind of a pattern there, I can't find it."

"There has to be some clue," says Alex. "Klondike left clues everywhere else."

"Hey—up there!" Rob cries, pointing. A sign above the targets reads:

> To win prize, hit:
> 1. every target with wings
> 2. every target that faces to the left
> 3. every target with two legs

"There's our next clue," Rob declares.

Jamal turns to Alex. "I guess it's show time. Alex, can you really hit all of those targets?" he asks.

"I think so," Alex replies.

Help Alex hit the targets. Follow Klondike's rules and cross out the targets that Alex should hit. The letters on the remaining targets will spell out a word for the puzzle in Klondike's Cavern.

WRITE DOWN THE ANSWER AND TURN TO CHAPTER 6, PAGE 20.

ITH WINGS 2) EVERY TARGET THAT FACES
3) EVERY TARGET WITH TWO LEGS
I R G A
O N R U
G P F E
P W S O

"I don't know," says Lenni. "There's something about this place. . . . Let's look some more."

"Aw, Lenni," Jamal groans. "What's to look at?"

Lenni's eyes rest on a map on the wall. It's very colorful, with fancy lettering and strange symbols.

"That's a nice map," Lenni remarks to Jesse.

Jesse nods. "Klondike did it. It's old, but I like keeping it around. It reminds me of him."

Jamal points to a picture on the wall. "Look. Isn't that the wax museum in the Fun House?"

"Yeah!" says Rob. "And that's the shooting gallery at Ride-O-Rama! Cool. The map is of Klondike's property."

"But what are those lines?" asks Gaby.

Tina is busy making a copy of the map in her notebook. "I'm drawing them in." She adds a question for Ghostwriter: "What are the lines on the map for?"

Suddenly Ghostwriter is back. Letters on the page start to move. Tina looks quickly to see if Jesse is watching. Ghostwriter is a secret—only members of the team can know about him. But Jesse is busy serving a customer.

"Hey," Tina whispers, "Ghostwriter's sending us a message!"

The team gathers around to see what he has written. Now the words say: A LINE CAN ALSO BE A ROAD.

"A road?" Jamal repeats. "But these lines aren't where the real roads are. And they crisscross like crazy."

"Like a maze!" Lenni suddenly shouts.

"What's like a maze?" asks Jesse, who's finished with his customer by now.

"These lines on the map," Lenni answers. "Come on, everyone, I bet we can solve this puzzle."

Help the team find their way through the maze. Start at the beginning and find the path that goes all the way through to the end. You can cross over symbols for the rides or the attractions, but you can't cross over pictures of hot dogs.

As you go through the paths, note the letters you pass over. When you reach the end, they'll spell out a word. Write the word on the blank spaces at the bottom of the page to complete an important message. Write the message in your casebook. You'll need it later in the story.

WHEN YOU'RE DONE, TURN TO CHAPTER 13, PAGE 41.

10

"We haven't tried door three yet," says Jamal. He pushes the bright blue door. It swings back with a squeak.

"Sounds spooky," says Tina, shivering.

By the light of Alex's flashlight, Jamal leads the team through a long hall that slopes upward. At the far end is a thick black curtain. Slowly Jamal pulls the curtain back and steps through the opening. His friends follow.

Candles flicker along the walls, dimly lighting what looks like a tunnel carved out of rock. Suddenly they hear someone laughing hysterically. "Ha, ha, ha!"

"What's that?" Gaby asks nervously.

"Maybe someone's watching us," Alex whispers.

Suddenly a huge, dark shape lurches out of the shadows.

"*Yaaaiii!*" Gaby ducks behind her brother.

The shape moves toward the team. Rob and Lenni jump back. Jamal shines Alex's flashlight on the figure's face. The light shows a wild-eyed woman with an evil smile.

"A w-witch!" Tina stammers.

"A *fake* witch. And she needs a nose job." Jamal peels some paint off the witch's hooked nose. "We're in the chamber of horrors, guys. It's all fake, don't worry."

"Yeah, chill, guys," Alex adds. But his voice is shaky.

The witch sinks back into the wall. The team walks by. Gaby makes sure that Alex is between her and the witch.

Suddenly Rob, who's in front, stops short. They're at a fork in the tunnel. There are four possible branches they can take.

"Which way do we go?" Rob asks.

"I say we keep going straight," Lenni offers.

Jamal shrugs. "Sounds good to me. Just keep looking for clues for the puzzle in Klondike's Cavern."

So the team heads into the branch of the tunnel that goes straight. It's dark, and they keep hearing spooky laughter. Sometimes it seems to be coming from behind them, and sometimes it seems to be coming from up ahead. Once a glowing bat swoops down from the ceiling at them.

"This chamber of horrors is scary enough for me," Gaby says to Tina.

"Hey! We're at another branch," calls Rob, who's still in the lead. "We have three choices of where to go."

"All these branches . . ." Lenni looks at Jamal. "Are you thinking what I'm thinking?"

Jamal nods. "Yup. Guys, I think we're in a maze!"

Get the team through the maze and out of the chamber of horrors. Here's the catch: There are four exits, but there's only one route that leads all the way from start to finish.

When you reach the correct exit, unscramble the letters you find there. You'll have another word for the puzzle in Klondike's Cavern.

WRITE DOWN THE ANSWER AND TURN TO CHAPTER 6, PAGE 20.

11

"Let's try door number two," says Gaby. She pushes open the door. On the other side is a ladder.

Gaby starts to climb and the rest of the team follows her. Soon they climb through a trapdoor into a room filled with bright lights and loud music.

Gaby grins. "Bumper cars!"

Empty multicolored bumper cars sit around a large hall. Red and blue neon lights flash, and music blares over a loudspeaker. Suddenly the doors open and a crowd of people streams toward the empty cars.

"What do we do now?" asks Tina.

"Let's go for a ride!" Rob says, laughing. The whole team runs to climb into the bumper cars.

"Got you!" Lenni shouts, crashing her car into Jamal's.

"Yeah!" yells Rob as he steers his car around the floor. "This is fun!"

"But how does it help us solve the puzzle?" Tina wants to know.

Alex steers up next to Tina. "Look for a clue."

"Hey," Jamal calls over the din. "The cars have letters on them! Maybe they're a clue."

"But how?" Tina asks.

"I think I know," says Rob. "Watch me!"

Help Rob solve this puzzle and find another word for the puzzle in Klondike's Cavern. Rob is in the bumper car at the top of the page. He has to get to the bottom of the page by bumping from one car to another. But he can only travel in the direction of the arrow on the car he just bumped. If there's more than one arrow, he can choose which way to go.

Each time Rob bumps a car, write down the letter on that car. By the time he reaches the bottom of the page, the letters should spell out a word. If they don't, go back to the top of the page and try a different route.

WRITE DOWN THE ANSWER AND TURN TO CHAPTER 6, PAGE 20.

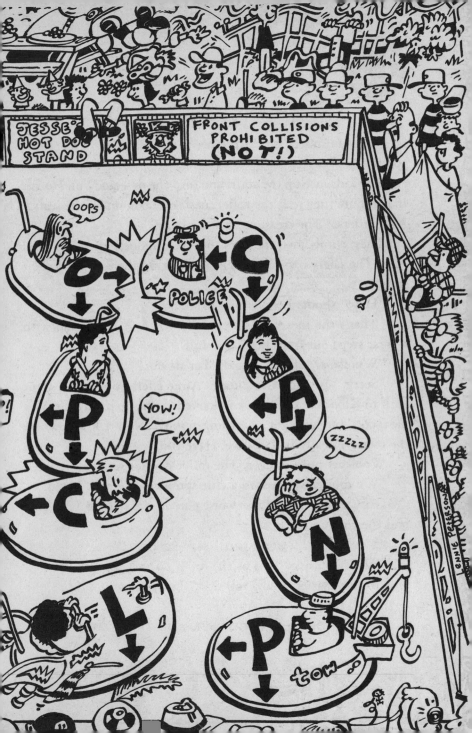

"The number is thirty-one," says Gaby. "The roller coaster!"

The kids race up the stairs and into the deserted Fun House. In a minute they're at the roller coaster. "Look under the seats," Alex orders. "The treasure must be here!"

They climb into the cars. All of a sudden there's a loud *clack*! The safety bars fall into place, locking the team into their seats.

"Hey!" shouts Lenni. "We're stuck!"

"That's the idea," says a gravelly voice. A large man with a cigar steps out from behind a wall.

"Woolcott!" shouts Jamal. "Let us out."

"Sorry." Woolcott snickers. "After I left you kids, I went back to Klondike's Cavern and looked at the puzzle again. You did good, but you got one thing wrong. Now I know where the treasure really is. Bye-bye! Have fun!"

Woolcott pulls a lever. The roller coaster starts to move.

"We must have missed a clue somewhere," says Jamal.

Gaby groans. "And the worst part is, we helped Woolcott find the treasure."

"That's not the worst part," says Lenni.

"What is?" asks Tina as the roller coaster tops a hill.

"Roller coasters make me sick," Lenni moans. *"Yeow!"*

END OF STORY—GO BACK AND TRY AGAIN!

"Okay," Lenni agrees. "Let's head for Ride-O-Rama."

"Be careful of that guy Woolcott," Jesse warns them. "I don't trust him."

The kids walk over to Ride-O-Rama. "Wow! This place sure has changed," says Alex as he gazes at the gleaming rides and the freshly painted buildings. Everything is new, except for a faded wooden shack right in the middle.

"That must be Klondike's old office," says Jamal.

"How can we get in to look around?" Tina asks.

Gaby knocks on the front door of the wooden building.

"Come in!" calls a man's gruff voice.

Gaby grins. "Follow me!"

They file into a dimly lit hallway. Through a door they see a messy office and a large man sitting behind a desk, chewing on a cigar and talking on the telephone.

"What do you kids want?" he growls.

"Are you Mr. Woolcott?" asks Gaby.

"Hold on," the man says into the phone. "Yeah, I am."

Gaby clears her throat. "We're doing a report for our school news show," she announces. "On famous clowns. We were wondering if we could see Klondike's old office."

"Klondike?" Mr. Woolcott sneers. "Who'd want to learn about him?" Then he stops talking to listen to the person on the phone.

"I know," he says angrily. "I'm looking for it!"

"So, can we look around?" asks Jamal.

"Huh?" Mr. Woolcott doesn't even look up. "Yeah, sure. His office was in the back. Just don't bother me."

"Thanks a lot!" Jamal pushes the rest of the team down the hallway.

"Did you hear?" Rob asks. "He's looking for something."

"Yeah," Alex answers. "I bet it's Klondike's fortune."

At the end of the hall they come to a wooden door. Jamal pushes it open. By the light of one bare bulb, they see that the room is piled high with clown gear. Giant shoes, masks, and baggy pants hang from the walls. Boxes of rubber noses and clown makeup are everywhere.

"Check this out," says Jamal. On the back wall is a sign that says: KLONDIKE'S CAVERN—FUNNY CLOWNS ONLY.

"Let's copy that," says Alex. "Maybe it's a clue."

Tina starts to write it in her notebook. Suddenly the letters on the page start to shimmer and move.

"Ghostwriter!" Tina whispers. "Hey, guys, look!"

When the letters stop moving, they spell out CAREFUL.

Rob laughs. "Careful of what? These rubber noses?"

Jamal leans against the sign. "It doesn't make—whoa!" He jumps away. The whole wall is moving!

"A secret passage!" Lenni cries. "Let's take it."

Rob frowns. "Ghostwriter said to be careful."

"We'll be careful," answers Lenni. She pushes the door open. "Come on."

TURN TO CHAPTER 3, PAGE 10.

WATCH IT! SOLVE IT! TELL A FRIEND!

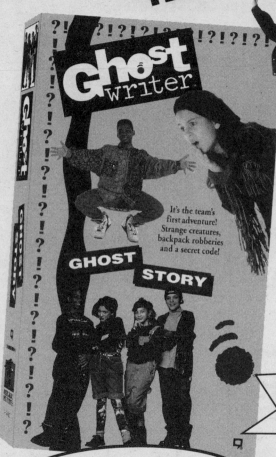

Ghostwriter Is Now Available On Videocassette!

$14.98* EACH
*Suggested Retail Price